DISCARD

P9-DGR-365

With love for Crash Bang Mark Barrett.
J. N.

Library of Congress Cataloging-in-Publication Data

Newton, Jill, 1964-
Crash Bang Donkey! / written and illustrated by Jill Newton.
p. cm.
Summary: A donkey's loud musical instruments annoy Farmer Gruff—until he discovers
that the music keeps away the pesky crows that have been eating his corn crop.
ISBN 978-0-8075-1330-9
[1. Noise—Fiction. 2. Music—Fiction. 3. Donkeys—Fiction. 4. Farm life—Fiction.] I. Title.
PZ7.N48674Cr 2010
[E]—dc22
2009025140

Text and illustrations copyright © 2010 by by Jill Newton.
Published in 2010 by Albert Whitman & Company,
6340 Oakton Street, Morton Grove, Illinois 60053-2723.
All rights reserved. No part of this book may be reproduced or transmitted in any form or by any means, electronic or mechanical,
including photocopying, recording, or by any information storage and retrieval system, without permission in writing from the publisher.
Printed in China.

10 9 8 7 6 5 4 3 2 HK 14 13 12 11 10 09

First published in Great Britain in 2010 by Gullane Children's Books.

For more information about Albert Whitman & Company, visit our web site at www.albertwhitman.com.

Crash Bang Donkey!

Jill Newton

Albert Whitman & Company, Chicago, Illinois

Farmer Gruff was a very happy man. There was just one thing wrong. Day and night, the crows munched and crunched on the corn in the cornfield, and day and night, Farmer Gruff had to chase them away.

R0426037778

Now he needed sleep, and he needed it badly! And while he slept, the animals made not a peep. The lambs skipped silently in the meadow, the pigs rolled silently in the mud, and the chickens laid eggs silently in the henhouse. There was not a sound to be heard, until . . .

CRASH! BANG!

A very noisy donkey
came over the hill.

"shush!"

whispered Pig
and Lamb and Chicken.
"Farmer Gruff is trying to sleep.
Your crashing and banging
will wake him up!"

But Donkey was making so
much noise he couldn't
hear them. He took out
his trumpet, and . . .

PARP!

he went.
"Please stop!"
clucked Chicken.
But Donkey *still*
couldn't hear.

PLINK PLONK PLONK PLINK!

"Come on, Pigster, feel the groove!"

"Ride the rhythm, baby!"

Then **POP!** Lamb pulled the plug.
"Hey dude, what's occurring?" cried Donkey.
"Aren't you digging my sounds?"
"You're making too much noise!" said Lamb.
"Farmer Gruff is asleep!"

"OK, guys, I hear you,"
said Donkey, and with a
Tra la la
he played a lullaby on his flute.
It didn't bang and it didn't crash . . .

But it was too late. Farmer Gruff wasn't asleep anymore. "Who's making all that NOISE?" he yelled. "Hey, Farmer G," said Donkey. "That would be me. I'm Crash Bang Donkey, and I'm here to play my music!"

"I can play the trombone,
toot the tuba,
blow the bagpipes,
and bash those bongos."

"Get in the groove, Gruffy!
It'll do you good!"

"I haven't got time
for music, Donkey,"
shouted Farmer Gruff.
"The crows are making a meal
of my corn, and YOU are making
me mad. Put that noise back in
your bag—and LEAVE!"

So Donkey left.

The animals went back to their quiet day, and Farmer Gruff
went back to sleep. But it wasn't long before a
CRASH BANG! CRASH BANG! came from the barn.
"Oh, no!" gasped Chicken and Pig and Lamb.
"Donkey's at it again!"

And then they noticed the crows. They were
flapping and squawking. Crash Bang Donkey
was scaring them away from the corn!

Chicken, Pig, and Lamb peered around the barn door.
"What's up?" exclaimed Donkey. "Was I too loud?
Did I make too much noise?"
"Oh, no!" said Pig with a grin.
"You made just the right amount
of noise," chuckled Chicken.
"I'm going to fetch Farmer Gruff!"
said Lamb excitedly.

Donkey looked worried.

But when Farmer Gruff saw the crows flapping
and squawking, he grinned.
"You can stay here after all, Donkey," he said.
"But you don't like my music!" said Donkey.
"Neither do the crows," said Farmer Gruff.
"There's a time to be quiet and a time to be loud.
And this is a time when you must
play as loudly as you can!"

And from that day forward, the crows didn't go anywhere near the corn, and Farmer Gruff got lots of sleep. Donkey even played him the occasional lullaby!